ALIEN FORCE

Sent from the planet Dijan, and now disguised as a normal schoolboy, Jodie's mission is to investigate and report why pollution levels are rising so fast on the planet Earth. In theory the mission is safe, but now Jodie's Calling Crystal is flashing a warning – there is a hostile alien force nearby and it has begun to track him down.

A fast-paced science fiction story with a strong environmental message.

Other Books by Theresa Breslin

Divided City (Random House)
The Dream Master (Random House)
Dream Master: Nightmare (Random House)
Dream Master: Gladiator (Random House)
Dream Master: Arabian Nights (Random House)
Simon's Challenge (Floris Books)
New School Blues (Floris Books)
Bullies at School (Floris Books)
Across the Roman Wall (Floris Books)
Starship Rescue (Barrington Stoke)
Alligator (Barrington Stoke)
Mutant (Barrington Stoke)
Whispers in the Graveyard (Egmont)

THERESA BRESLIN

Illustrated by Bob Harvey

BARN OWL BOOKS

BARN OWL BOOKS
157 Fortis Green Road, London, N10 3LX

First Published in 1995 by Puffin Books

This edition Barn Owl Books, 2008
157 Fortis Green Road, London, N10 3LX

Distributed by Frances Lincoln,
4 Torriano Mews, Torriano Avenue, London, NW5 2RZ

ISBN 978 19 0 301575 9

Designed and typeset by Skandesign Limited
Printed in the UK by CPI Cox and Wyman, Reading, RG1 8EX

CHAPTER ONE

DANGER!

Clear and distinct came the warning signal inside Jodie's receiving cell.

DANGER!

His hand grasped his pencil and he stopped writing. He listened. Now there was only silence, a hollow echo inside his head. He could hear his heart thudding, and also … the other sound still lingering in his ears. He waited. Had he been mistaken?

He raised his head and glanced around him. All his classmates were bent over their test papers scribbling furiously.

DANGER … DANGER …

There it was again. Jodie looked up quickly. No doubt now what it was. An alarm call, the agreed intergalactic alert signal, and it was being directed at him. He frowned.

Mr Neil, his teacher, noticed, and gave him an encouraging smile. Since Jodie was a resident at the local Children's Home, most of the teachers at Bishop Primary School were extra helpful to him. It was embarrassing sometimes.

Adam Caldwell, who sat opposite Jodie, saw

6

Mr Neil's look. He put his tongue out and made licking motions like a cat lapping milk.

'Suck up to teacher,' he whispered.

Mr Neil came over.

'Need any help, Jodie?' he asked kindly.

Jodie shook his head. If only Mr Neil knew. Far from needing any help with the test Jodie could have completed it, with all answers correct, in the time that it took the rest of the class to write their names. But Jodie always worked slowly and made mistakes. The kind of mistakes that any ordinary eleven-year-old might make.

Except that he probably wasn't eleven years old.

And he certainly wasn't ordinary.

Jodie didn't know how old he was exactly. Where he came from time wasn't measured in days or years. He had not yet fully matured, he knew that. He was still in the junior forming process of the people of the planet Dijan, known as the GuardRings.

From far off in space the GuardRings had watched with increasing sadness the slow decline of this once beautiful water planet, strangely named Earth by those who dwelt on it. Greed, stupidity and

selfishness had already combined to pollute the water and threaten the life-giving rain forests. Now the contamination seemed to be reaching into the minds and hearts of the people themselves.

The GuardRings had begun to wonder what was pushing forward the destruction of Earth.

'The Earth People have the means and money to harness natural energy, yet they squander it on arms and war machines,' Jodie's own father had stated at the High Council. 'They need our guidance.'

'It is not our policy to interfere in the affairs of other beings,' said Ronsard, the Senate Leader.

'Have you forgotten the very purpose of our existence?' cried the eldest Senator in the Council room. He rose to his feet. 'Have you forgotten our own history? Many suns ago, we of the planet Dijan were appointed as the GuardRings of the Galaxy. We arbitrate in disagreements between worlds. We assist when famine and disaster strikes. We must send a Traveller onto Earth to help them.' He raised his hands in the air. 'And soon,' he said.

'We do not go unless we are summoned,' persisted Ronsard.

'They do not know to ask,' said Jodie's

father sadly.

Jodie's father was responsible for training the Travellers, the élite force who journeyed among the stars to help those who lived on other planets.

'The Council will wait too late to send someone,' he had said to Jodie later as they studied on their monitoring screens the damage being done to Earth's atmosphere. 'Global warming, nuclear tests, they will kill themselves and harm us all.' He pressed the control panel and studied Earth's ozone layer more closely. 'Why can't they see what they are doing?' He shook his head. 'What makes them ignore what is happening to their planet? Why do Earth people allow such pollution?'

It was then that Jodie decided to volunteer to come and live among the humans. 'I'll observe and report back to you, father,' he said. 'And if an emergency arises I will be there to help.'

And now he was actually here on Earth. He had never imagined it would be so difficult to adjust to the lifestyle of the Earth people. Jodie looked around his classroom again. Of all the worlds he had visited, it was one of the most strange. Everyone's mind seemed closed and shuttered. He probed gently outwards with his own. Adam's thoughts were hostile and aggressive, the rest of his fellow pupils worried and anxious about getting low marks in their exam. And another mind near by ... Jodie recoiled in surprise. Some other person close to him had also been thought travelling.

DANGER ... DANGER ...

The high-pitched sonic note sounded once more in the tiny receiving cell of his inner ear. He was being signalled urgently.

WARNING ...

Jodie went on writing, filling out his answers with one hand. The fingers of his other hand moved towards his pencil case, where his star-shaped Calling Crystal lay hidden. Five points in the star. Five coloured codes to give him information. From the paler pinks and greens of the standard information relays, to the darker shades of the more urgent messages.

DANGER ...

He unzipped the pencil case and, taking out his rubber, erased one of his answers. The Crystal lay

11

among the leaky biros, the sharpener and the pencil shavings. He pressed his thumb on the digital square at its centre and, as his personal print registered, the message meant for him pulsated throughout its shape.

His eyes widened in fright as its colour went from white to blue, then lilac, through to indigo.

Unnoticed by Jodie, Adam Caldwell leaned forward to see what he was doing. Jodie didn't feel his presence. His mind was completely focused on the Crystal, which now glowed with a deep purple light.

Jodie stared at it in shock. Not since there had been a malfunction in one of the artificial suns of the planet Seya, and the GuardRings had been summoned to prevent it plunging down on their capital city, had Jodie seen a message with so deep a colour.

Louder now, and, it seemed to him, right inside his head, the alert vibrated.

DANGER …

… Across the vast void of space, into the dense atmosphere of Earth, down through the stratosphere, homing in on his Crystal …

WARNING …

Out from beyond the seven silent planets

someone was trying desperately to contact him. Curving round the galaxy, past the pulsars and through the drifting Milky Way the message came.

BEWARE …

He was in deadly danger.

But from where and from whom?

CHAPTER TWO

There was a sharp clatter as Adam Caldwell fell on the floor. He had been leaning so far out into the passageway beside his desk that his chair had tipped right over, and he landed sprawling at Jodie's feet.

Jodie switched off the Crystal and hurriedly closed his pencil case. Had Adam caught sight of the glowing star?

He reached his hand out to help Adam to his feet.

'Leave me alone, you!' said Adam angrily.

He kicked Jodie's school bag viciously as he stood up.

Jodie watched Adam as he sat down again. Why was he so annoyed? Jodie tried to work out a reason. Adam had fallen down in front of the whole class. He had been humiliated and that had made him aggressive, so had had kicked out. But he had also been hostile to Jodie on other occasions. In fact, Adam had always seemed antagonistic towards him, since Jodie's first day in the school. On Dijan everyone was trained from their birth-time to think before acting in anger. These Earth people were very impulsive. Their minds were …

Jodie gasped.

There it was again! A gentle turning in his own mind, no more than a bubble of air rising to the surface in a glass of water. Except he hadn't put it there. Someone else had. A thought traveller.

Somewhere, close to him, another being was reaching out a silken ribbon of thought, probing and seeking … what?

The classroom door opened. The Headteacher stood in the doorway. Beside her was a young girl, dark-skinned, dark-haired and pretty. She was wearing silk trousers of the palest green, softly cuffed at her ankles, and a matching embroidered top. A beautiful

16

multi-coloured sari was draped around her body. In her fingers she held a sequinned scarf, which had small silver shapes of moons and stars stitched to it. It sparkled as it caught the light.

'I want to introduce a new pupil to the class,' said the Head. 'Her name is Kali. I would like you all to make her most welcome to Bishop Primary School.'

The Head's gaze moved around the classroom. She stopped when she reached Jodie. She stared hard at him. He felt his face become hot and he dropped his eyes.

'Those of you who are fairly new to the school themselves could perhaps make a special effort,' the Head continued. She gave Kali a place to sit and turned to speak to Mr Neil.

Jodie took advantage of those few moments to glance about quickly. The person who was telepathic must surely be in the room. He tried to find clues in the faces which surrounded him.

Who was it?

Most of his classmates were rushing to finish their test paper. Adam had completed his and was chewing the end of his pencil. Kali sat looking with interest at everything. When their eyes met she returned Jodie's gaze steadily and calmly. Was it her? Her face was serene. With great determination Jodie prevented his thoughts from moving outwards. If they did, and connected with the other thought traveller, then he or she might lock on to his mind. They would learn his identity and know right away that he, Jodie, was different.

He shivered. This mind was so close beside him, so very close that he could sense its agitated hum. Buzzing and flitting within the room, Jodie felt it to be a peculiar type of brain pattern. It seemed to him more than just another being seeking communication. There was something not normal about these ESP waves.

They were violent and dangerous.

He sat motionless in his chair and concentrated. Then a cold chill of fear descended on him as he realized the truth. The mind he could sense was a mind whose sole purpose was destruction.

The bell rang for the end of the school day. Jodie started, and then, with his head bent, he tidied his exam sheets. He hurriedly gathered his belonging and put them in his school bag. He had to get back to his room at the Children's Home and set up the communication line on his computer. He needed to find out why his father was sending him such an urgent signal from Dijan.

'Would you see Kali across the main road, please?' Mr Neil stopped Jodie as he was leaving the classroom. 'She has moved into the flats on the other side and as she is new to Scotland everything must be quite unusual for her.'

Jodie tried to smile as they walked along the corridor together. He *had* to get home as quickly as possible, to receive whatever transmission was being sent out. Kali was trotting beside him, trying to keep up. As they reached the entrance hall she put her hand on his arm.

'Must we go so fast?' she asked him. 'I am quite tired out. I find everything here so different from my own country.'

'Yes, it is a strange place to live,' said Jodie. 'Some of their customs are so odd...'

He stopped speaking as he realized what he had said. Kali gave him an inquiring look.

'So you are not Scottish?' she asked him. 'I *thought* your accent was not the same as the others. Where do you come from?'

Jodie hesitated. She was very observant. 'Down south, I think,' he stammered. 'I live at the Children's Home.'

Kali touched his arm again.

'I didn't mean to be impolite,' she said.

Jodie shrugged. 'It's OK,' he said.

His father had chosen wisely when he had decided on a background of a Children's Home for Jodie. It had been complicated to hack into official computer systems and alter records, but it had been worth it. Nobody questioned Jodie closely, and it explained away any strangeness in his manner.

As they went outside, Kali put on her scarf and wound it round her neck. They reached the dual carriageway, and, as they waited for the lollipop lady to return from the other side, Adam came up close behind Kali.

'You'll need to wrap up warmer than that when the snow comes,' he said, pulling at her scarf.

'Snow!' exclaimed Kali. 'Snow! I've never seen snow. I can't wait.'

Adam frowned at her. This wasn't the reaction he'd expected.

'I hope you're not going to be eating smelly curries,' he said, holding his nose.

'They do pong a bit, don't they?' Kali laughed. 'My favourite food is fish and chips.' She smiled at Adam and looked directly into his eyes. 'What's yours?'

Adam kicked a stone out into the road.

'Pizza,' he mumbled. 'Deep fried.'

They crossed the road in a group. Adam and Kali started talking.

'I'll walk with you, if you like,' offered Adam.

'These flats look all the same. I know when we first moved in I kept getting lost.'

Jodie could hardly believe it. He had tried unsuccessfully to make friends with Adam weeks ago and now Kali, after only some minutes of meeting and despite Adam's initial rudeness, was chatting away to him. It was as if she had bewitched him.

As Adam and Kali turned towards the flats, Jodie waved goodbye and ran across the park to the Children's Home. It was built in the shape of a large X, with four separate 'houses' meeting at the centre in a large games hall. Jodie opened the back door of his house unit and slipped through. His room was on the first floor. He headed towards the stairs. Suddenly a voice called out sharply behind him.

'Hey, where are you off to?'

CHAPTER THREE

'Hi, Jodie. Why are you in such a rush tonight?' It was Albert, one of the house parents, who had stepped out from the kitchen.

'Em…' Jodie pointed to his school bag. 'I've work to do on my project.'

'Bet you haven't,' said Albert kindly, putting his hand on Jodie's shoulder. 'Bet you're racing upstairs to play on that daft computer. Come on in and have a cup of tea with the rest of us.'

Reluctantly Jodie followed him into the kitchen and sat down at the big table.

'Look who I've captured,' said Albert. He

poured some hot tea into a mug. 'The one and only Jodie.'

'Thanks.' Jodie took the mug and sipped at the liquid. It had taken him some time to become accustomed to this habit of the Earth people. They drank this unusual combination of leaves, water, sugar and animal milk frequently, and at any time of the day.

'We've missed you, haven't we, kids?' Albert asked Ellie and Grace. Beanie, the littlest boy who was just five, was slumped asleep in his chair, thumb in mouth.

Jodie smiled nervously. This was the most tricky part of his Earth-life – behaving naturally in company. He was usually quiet and watchful, and this worked well at school. Most times everyone in the classroom was busy working and the playground was always noisy, so it was easy for him to blend in. At the Children's Home there were fewer people and Albert was there to notice things.

'You don't join in any of the group activities, Jodie,' Albert went on. 'You're spending far too much time in front of that screen. Do you know,' he addressed the other children at the table, 'I actually heard him talking to his computer last night when I passed his bedroom door?'

Jodie's hand shook. He put his cup down. What had Albert heard him saying? Jodie tried to recall his conversation of the previous evening with his father. He would need to be more careful. Did Albert suspect him of having a secret to hide?

'Jodie?' Albert had asked him a question.

'Sorry. What did you say?' Jodie tried to smile casually.

'Honestly, Jodie. Sometimes you seem miles away. I think maybe I should take the plug off your computer so that you can't use it. That might improve your concentration.'

Jodie looked at Albert. Was he joking or was there something more sinister behind his friendly smile?

'No. No, please,' Jodie said quickly. 'You're right. I will spend more time with everyone else. In fact,' he stood up, 'why don't we play a game right now?'

Ellie laughed out loud. 'You can do what you like, Jodie. *I'm* going to watch my soap on the telly before dinner.'

'Me too,' said Grace, and she stood up from her chair and followed Ellie through to the lounge.

'I'll play with you, Jodie,' said a small voice.

Beanie had woken up. He gazed up at Jodie, his big brown eyes pleading and hopeful.

'Sure,' said Jodie. 'Want a game of football in the yard?'

Beanie nodded, slid off his chair, and ran to get the ball.

'That's kind of you, Jodie,' said Albert quietly. He picked up the mugs and rinsed them in the sink. 'I'll start making dinner while you train Beanie for the World Cup Squad.'

Jodie knew that Beanie had stayed in the Children's Home since he was a baby. Some children were long-stay, like Ellie, whose mother had died and whose father had gone back to Trinidad for a while. Some came and went for all sorts of reasons. Grace's mum was in hospital for a major operation and there was no one else to look after her.

All the young people mixed in and helped with the chores, but Jodie rarely played with the rest. The reason was straightforward. He simply didn't know how to.

26

At his real home, on Dijan, he had applied and been selected to train as a Traveller who might be sent on intergalactic missions. It was huge honour but the studying was very difficult. Most of his life had been spent in learning about the many nations, civilizations and religions which existed throughout the Universe. The Dijans used brain information implants which Jodie could reel through if he needed a particular fact. Special tutors had perfected his skills in reasoning and practical technology. There had been little time for recreation.

So, although Jodie could, with a moment's reflection, recite accurately the rules of soccer, when it came to actually playing the game he was hopeless. Very soon Beanie began to outplay him. Jodie could see Albert watching them from the kitchen window as he peeled the potatoes. He was glad when they were eventually called in for dinner.

'I like playing football with Jodie,' said Beanie, as Albert put his dinner in front of him.

'I'm not surprised,' said Albert and he winked at Jodie. 'You must have been trying extra hard to play as badly as that,' he murmured as he passed Jodie's chair.

It was Jodie's turn to help with the clearing away and washing up and, as he did so, he heard again the warning bleep in his inner ear. It seemed fainter and less distinct, but still insistent. His father wanted him to call in. He walked past the lounge. The door was open. Albert was helping Beanie with his reading and Grace and Ellie were playing cards. Jodie called through the open door.

'I'm tired. I think I'll go upstairs to bed.'

Albert smiled and waved goodnight.

In the safety of his own room, Jodie took the Calling Crystal from his bag, keyed in the number code, and fitted it into the back of his computer. He switched it on. Almost immediately the image of his father appeared on the screen. He spoke at once.

'Traveller Jodie of Dijan,' he said, 'you are in great danger.'

CHAPTER FOUR

Without realizing what he was doing, Jodie reached out and touched his father's face on the screen in front of him.

His father smiled and lifted his hand in greeting.

'My son,' he said softly.

Jodie blinked and looked down at the keyboard.

'Traveller Jodie of Dijan ready to receive message,' he said.

'Listen with attention to what I have to say to you,' said his father, 'for I believe that your life is at risk.'

Jodie raised his head and stared at his father's face.

'You know the story of our galaxy, Jodie,' his father continued, 'how we came to be encircled by the seven silent planets. This was after the final nuclear wars, when Dijan was the last world left in our solar system which could sustain life. All the others lie barren and empty; wastelands where nothing will ever grow again.'

Jodie's father sighed as he remembered the

years of destruction and chaos.

'We took a solemn vow never to let this happen again, and to help others to live in peace and safety. So our world and our people became the GuardRings of the Galaxy. However, all the discord and chaos were not due solely to the stupidity and greed of frail mortal beings. The history records you studied as a young child which told of an malevolent Alien Force were not star stories made up to frighten young Dijans.'

He paused and then went on.

'There is such a being - an Alien which feeds on negative impulses. Think of it as similar to a black hole in space, sucking in other life forms. Feeding on organic matter. It encourages discord and destruction in order to survive. Its goal? Ultimate chaos.'

Jodie leaned forward as he heard the change in the voice transmitted over light-years. Was his father afraid?

'Traveller Jodie, I have to tell you that we believe the Alien Force has arrived on planet Earth.'

The sound coming through the Calling Crystal crackled and the computer screen distorted. Jodie altered the settings to tune in again.

'You will return to Dijan and we will send a greater number of more experienced Travellers onto Earth.'

Black zig-zag lines covered the screen and then it went blank. Faintly Jodie could hear his father's voice.

'Please be vigilant while you are awaiting your transport to leave. The Alien must never gain possession of the Calling Crystal…Even now… close… Take utmost care… may know of your presence… Guard the Crystal with your life.'

A burst of static sounded in Jodie's ear. Then silence. He tried in vain to reconnect. The transmission had been broken. Suddenly the screen flickered again and words appeared. Jodie was confused. This hadn't happened in the past. They had always communicated by vision and sound. He read the message slowly.

EMERGENCY CONTACT. EMERGENCY CONTACT. COME IMMEDIATELY WITH CRYSTAL TO ELECTRICAL POWER STATION AT EDGE OF TOWN. THERE YOU WILL RECEIVE FURTHER INSTRUCTION.

Jodie had never seen anything like this before. More words appeared on the screen.

BELIEVE NORMAL COMMUNICATION CHANNELS BEING MONITORED. COME NOW. HURRY.

Jodie jumped up from his chair and pulled on his jacket. He removed the Crystal from his computer. Then he crept down the stairs and let himself out of the back door.

He reckoned it would take him ten minutes to get to the power station. He ran fast, keeping in the shadow of the trees on the fringes of the park, the Crystal clutched in his hand.

The power station was deserted when he arrived. He could hear a dog barking far away. Despite the secure entry gates and high fence it would only take him a small space of time to get in. If he let his fingers rest on the keypad and concentrated hard he should be able to sense the correct number combination. He moved the Crystal into his other hand and reached out to touch the electronic lock.

There was the faintest of bleeps in the sonic sounder in his ear. He paused. His father had always told him he was too impulsive, rushing to do things when he should stop and think. He looked at the Crystal lying in the palm of his hand. Very carefully

he brushed the centre with his thumb print. Immediately it turned deep purple and became warm in his hand.

Jodie stared at it in alarm.

DANGER!

Jodie whirled round, switched off the Crystal, and raced for safety among the trees in the park. There was a loud crash of thunder and a brilliant shock of lightning lit up the sky. Jodie looked back. Flashes of electricity surged along the steel frame of the gate. He must keep running. He looked round him wildly for some cover. Just ahead were some shrubs and rhododendron bushes. He plunged among them, then crawled swiftly as far as could into the centre of a vast clump of greenery. As soon as he reached the middle he changed direction and came out on one of the walkways near the pond. He forced himself to keep his mind blank and walk casually back to the Children's Home.

It had been a trap. Jodie realized that now. He would have walked straight through the gate towards whatever was waiting for him, with his Crystal switched off and completely defenceless, because he thought it was some friendly message from Dijan.

And the Alien had known that. It was aware that a Dijan Traveller was on Earth and it sought the power that the Crystal could give. He, Jodie, could have been captured or killed and the Crystal taken. He had ignored his father's warning and had rushed off without thinking. A snare had been set for him, and he had almost got caught.

His heart was still hammering when he sneaked into his house unit some fifteen minutes later. The door of Albert's office was open. As he passed by, Jodie could see that it was empty. Albert must be in the main hall, thought Jodie, or seeing to one of the other children. He walked upstairs and opened the door of his own room. He went inside and closed it behind him.

Jodie took one pace forwards and then stood completely still. All his senses were alert. His room was not empty as he had left it.

He could hear quiet movement in front of him.

There was someone there. Someone in his room.

CHAPTER FIVE

Jodie felt real fear racing through his body.

He was alone, unprotected, and light-years from home and safety. Near to him someone was breathing quietly. He stepped back, and as he did so he heard a whimper.

He stopped. The light from the street lamp outside showed a figure lying on his bed. A very small figure.

'Beanie?' Jodie whispered.

Beanie opened his eyes and sat up.

'What are you doing here?' said Jodie. 'What's wrong?'

'I had a bad dream,' said Beanie in a scared little voice. 'It was dark and I was cold.'

Jodie took off his jacket and picked Beanie up.

'Come on,' he said. 'I'll carry you back to your own bed and tell you a story until you fall asleep.'

Telling Beanie stories helped calm Jodie down. Later he would think about what had happened today. Then he could sort out the information logically and try to fit all the pieces together.

'Another story,' Beanie mumbled in a tired voice.

Jodie began to recite a Dijan limerick.

> *'There once was a Kamar of Kroo,*
> *Who lived all alone in the zoo—'*

'What's a Kamar?' demanded Beanie.

'It's a bit like an Earth elephant,' said Jodie, 'only smaller and it has green fur. Now listen and don't interrupt.'

> *'There once was a Kamar of Kroo,*
> *Who lived all alone in the zoo,*
> *Now he shouldn't have oughter,*
> *Eaten the zoo-keeper's daughter.*
> *But...*
> *He was hungry, so, what else could he do?'*

Soon Beanie fell asleep, thumb happily in his mouth. Jodie tucked him in and returned to his own room.

He took the Calling Crystal from his pocket and turned it over and over in his hand. He didn't dare connect it up to his computer for he now knew with absolute certainty that his communications were being monitored. Jodie thought carefully. It could only be the incoming messages which had been intercepted. If his outgoing ones had been traced, then the Alien would have known where he was and come here to his room to destroy him and take the Crystal. That was why the false message had been put on the screen asking him to go to the power station. It was because his exact location was not known.

'So,' Jodie spoke softly to himself, 'for the moment I am safe.'

He looked at the Calling Crystal. It was white and silent. From now on it would have to remain like that. If he pressed its centre even once more to receive a message the Alien would trace him immediately. He felt very alone.

As he lay under his duvet, Jodie backtracked again through the events of the day. Was there something obvious which he had missed earlier? Suddenly he remembered the strange sensation that he had experienced in the school classroom. Someone had been reaching outwards with their mind. The other pupils had not noticed as they did not possess telepathic gifts. But he had. And could recognize it for what it was: transmitted brainwaves. Jodie sat up in bed. They had been of an extremely disturbed type – the thought patterns of the Alien!

But *who was it?*

Perhaps someone who sat right beside him! What if their minds had actually linked…? Jodie clenched his teeth. He would have been revealed without doubt. He would not now be snug and warm in bed.

'Who could it be?'

In the darkness of his room he spoke the question aloud.

Adam? Hostile and angry.

The Headteacher? She had stared at him until he had felt compelled to drop his gaze. Had she caught the tail end of his psychic thoughts and recognized them?

Or it could have been from further away.

Someone in the Children's Home? Someone who knew he spent a lot of his time on his computer?

Who?

Jodie lay back down and cleared his mind to prepare for sleep. There was something else, though … hesitant and elusive, just outside his fully conscious thought. And, as he slid into his dream-time, it rose up out of his learning memory bank. To prepare himself for

his work on Earth he had absorbed as much information as possible about the culture and beliefs of the inhabitants. A single fact connected with another in his brain.

One of this world's major religions had a deity who was devoted to destruction and chaos.

A Hindu goddess.

Her name…

'Kali,' Jodie murmured in his sleep.

CHAPTER SIX

Jodie woke early the next morning and went downstairs. Albert was already in the kitchen making toast.

'Didn't you sleep well?' he asked Jodie.

'Fine.' Jodie watched him as he bustled around the kitchen. Was it his imagination or was Albert behaving in an anxious way?

'I thought I heard someone up and about late last night.' Albert set out the boxes of cereals, bowls and spoons on the table.

'Beanie had a nightmare,' said Jodie, helping himself to some toast. 'I took him back to bed and told him some stories.'

'Good stories,' said Beanie, running into the kitchen still in his pyjamas. He climbed up onto his chair. Jodie poured out milk and cereal for him and gave him his spoon.

'Do you have bad dreams, Jodie?' Albert asked.

'No,' Jodie said quickly.

Albert smiled at him. 'Everybody does,' he said. 'Perhaps you just don't remember yours, or choose not to.'

Jodie gave him a long look. What did Albert mean? What was he thinking of? Was he genuinely concerned for Jodie or was there another more insidious reason for his questions?

'Poems too,' said Beanie, interrupting. He munched his cereal. 'Jodie told me poems. Tell Albert about the Kamar, Jodie.'

Jodie stared at the little boy. How did he know one of the animals native to Dijan? Then he remembered. Last night, foolishly, without thinking, he had recited some limericks from his own childhood.

'A Kamar?' Albert laughed. 'What's a Kamar?'

'It's a bit like an Earth elephant,' said Beanie importantly, ''cept it's got green fur. That's right, isn't it, Jodie?'

'I was telling him some nonsense verse.' Jodie laughed nervously. 'Come on,' he took Beanie's hand, 'you're still in your PJs. I'll help you get dressed.' He dragged Beanie out of the room. As he glanced back over his shoulder he could see Albert watching them both with a puzzled expression on his face.

In school, Jodie found that he couldn't concentrate on his work.

'I don't know where your mind is today, Jodie,' joked Mr Neil, 'but it doesn't seem to be in my classroom.'

Jodie raised his eyes to Mr Neil's face. Did the teacher's remark about his mind have a special significance? He rubbed his forehead, hard. This was ridiculous. He was beginning to suspect everyone around him. Adults and his fellow pupils.

He recalled his thought before falling asleep last night and he looked across to where Kali was sitting. It couldn't be her. She was gazing at him, a sympathetic look in her eyes. As a foreigner to this country she was treated almost like an alien by some of the school pupils. Why did people do that? If you had unusual clothes or speech you could become a target for comments and cruel remarks. He had noticed Kali far ahead of him on his way to school earlier. She was being followed by a small group of children who were calling names and pointing at her. She had hurried to get into the school building. Was it a crime to be different?

Jodie was glad when the bell for lunch break finally rang. He went and sat by himself on the playground wall. From here he could see across the road to the park and, further in the distance, to the electricity power station. The coils of the distributors and transformers were outlined against the sky. The power which they contained flowed and surged there daily to keep up with the demand from the nearby town which needed heat and light for the many houses, offices and shops.

Why had the Alien chosen that particular place for the trap? It hadn't been an accidental selection. It was connected in some way with the power source. Concentrated electrical fields could block out radio waves and brain waves. They would mask any type of activity of that kind. Then Jodie realized why. For the Alien it would be like wearing a black cloak on a dark night. That was why he, Jodie, had walked so unsuspectingly right up to the gate. His extrasensory perception had been blocked and had not alerted him to any sense of danger as he had approached.

But perhaps there was also another reason that the power station had been picked for the meeting place. Some more important reason … to do with accessing a source of energy.

If only he could contact Dijan. They would tell him what to do. Suddenly Jodie missed his father very much.

He blinked and let his gaze wander to where a group of children were playing. Kali stood awkwardly and alone, just outside a circle of chatting friends. Her dress and nationality made her conspicuous, it highlighted that she was not the same as the rest. She always appeared so calm, thought Jodie, but maybe she wasn't. It must be scary for her to be here in a land where the weather was so much cooler, people's skins were so much lighter and few spoke her language. Where was Adam? He seemed to have appointed himself as her protector. Surely he would come into the playground and speak to her?

Jodie's eyes flicked back towards the school building. The new start infants were going home. Albert was going into the school to collect Beanie. He

waved over to Jodie. Jodie waved back, and then his eyes moved along the line of classrooms at the front. His own faced out into the playground. He could see right into his classroom from here. It was empty because everyone was taking their break.

But no, not completely empty. Not everyone was outside. One person wasn't in the playground. There was a figure in the classroom. It was bent over Jodie's desk. Who could it be? What were they doing?

Jodie straightened up in horror. It was Adam Caldwell, and he had something in his hand.

It was Jodie's pencil case.

CHAPTER SEVEN

Jodie raced across the playground. He almost knocked Kali over in his haste. He had to stop Adam – had to reach him before he took the Calling Crystal. If Adam handled it at all then he would know that it was special and might show it to others.

As Jodie entered the school he collided with the Headteacher. She was helping to supervise the infant class dismissal.

'Young man,' she said severely. 'More haste less speed.' Then, as he did not stop, she called after him angrily, 'Come back here at once!'

If anything, Jodie ran faster. He wrenched open the classroom door just as Adam lifted the Calling

Crystal out of the pencil case.

'Don't touch that!'

Jodie strode across the room. He faced Adam directly. 'It's mine,' he said. 'Give it to me.'

Adam laughed and held the Crystal high up, out of Jodie's reach.

'Make me,' he sneered.

'Yes,' Jodie said firmly. 'I will.' Bringing his psychic powers together to the front of his mind, Jodie concentrated his thoughts outwards and forward. He reached deep into the left-hand lobe of Adam's brain and triggered the motor impulse which controlled the hand movement. As if in a dream,

Adam lowered his arm, and holding the Crystal in the palm of his hand he offered it to Jodie.

Jodie reached out to take it.

At that precise moment the Headteacher marched into the classroom.

'Jodie. I want to speak to you this minute!' she snapped.

Adam blinked and looked down at his hand. He made to close his fingers and pull away, just as Jodie tried to snatch the Crystal from him. Their hands collided, and the Crystal spun up into the air. Slowly, slowly it tumbled down. Jodie snatched at it desperately but it slipped through his grasp and onto the floor.

As if from far away, Jodie heard the bell sound for the end of lunch break. The next few minutes were complete confusion. Mr Neil came into the room. Within a few moments the rest of the class were there, pushing and jostling to see what was happening. Kali slipped forward and stood at Jodie's side.

He bent down and started scrabbling under the desks and chairs.

'Jodie, stand up!' said the Headteacher sharply. 'Right now!'

'An explanation from both boys might be in

order,' said Mr Neil.

'I agree,' said the Head. 'If you attend to your class I will interview them in my office.' She spoke to Adam and Jodie. 'Follow me,' she ordered as she left the room.

Jodie gave one last despairing look over the classroom floor. He could see nothing at all. His Calling Crystal had completely disappeared.

'How did you do that?' said Adam as they followed the Head along the corridor.

'What?' said Jodie blankly.

'You know. The trick with my arm. Making me give you the little star thing. Are you a hypnotist or what?'

Jodie didn't answer right away. Adam wasn't the Alien. He knew that for sure. Otherwise he wouldn't have been able to control him so easily. And Adam's mind, despite a large amount of aggressive thought, was actually quite innocent. But he needed an explanation for what had happened. So why not give him the one he himself had suggested?

'Yeah,' mumbled Jodie. 'Sort of.'

'Wow!' said Adam in admiration. 'I knew you were kind of weird when I first saw you, but I didn't realize you could hypnotize people.'

'Is that why you didn't make friends?' asked Jodie bitterly. 'Because you thought I was weird?'

'Me? Not make friends?' said Adam in surprise. 'I spoke to you the first day you arrived. You didn't even answer me. Just walked away talking to yourself. You do that all the time. It's a real turn-off.'

'Do I?" said Jodie. And then he realized that he *had* acted stand-offish on his first days at school. Afraid of rebuffs, he'd pretended it didn't matter whether anyone talked to him or not. He'd been awkward and abrupt. 'I didn't realize,' he said. Then after a moment he added, 'Sorry.'

'Anyway,' said Adam, 'we'd better think up our story mega-fast.' He nodded towards the Head, walking swiftly down the corridor in front of them.

'A game?' suggested Jodie.

'Yeah,' said Adam. 'Let's say we were playing seek-and-find, and you got carried away. Act up a bit about being new and not coping and stuff. And take that superior look off your face,' he advised as they followed the Head into her office.

Twenty minutes later they were back outside, with a punishment exercise each to do for tomorrow, and yard sweeping duties for a week.

Jodie was anxious for the rest of the afternoon. His Crystal was gone. Someone must have picked it up. Would whoever it was appreciate its vast power? Would they play with it and perhaps manage to activate it in some way? It was in itself a small gravity-defying piece of white glass, but connected in the correct manner to other electrical equipment it could enhance their function enormously. A force for good in the Universe – when in the right hands. In the wrong hands ... Jodie shuddered.

Also, something else was happening which was causing him real distress. The barrier he'd erected to block off telepathic communication was under siege. Jodie's brief journey into Adam's mind had made it more difficult for him to keep his thoughts on a regular Earth human pattern.

And ... someone knew this. Knew because they had picked up the telepathic thought transfer in the classroom earlier. Not certain who had done it, but knew that it had happened and was searching for the origin. A disturbed mind with havoc as its aim. Watching and waiting for him to slip up again.

Moving closer and closer.

CHAPTER EIGHT

As soon as the playground had cleared after the final bell, Jodie slipped back into his classroom. He began a thorough search of the room, inside each desk, on the chairs, on the floor. A few minutes later Adam appeared.

'You're looking for your little star, aren't you? He said. 'Do you need it for your hypnosis?'

'It's much more important than that,' Jodie snapped.

'I'll help you look for it if you teach me how to do that trick,' said Adam.

'It's not a cheap trick.' Worry made Jodie speak recklessly. 'You are so stupid you didn't know that what you held in your hand was unique. It could mean the saving of your planet.'

Adam laughed.

'I don't believe you,' he said.

'I do,' said a voice from the door.

The boys looked up from where they had been kneeling on the floor. Kali stood in the doorway.

'What do you know?' Jodie asked her suspiciously.

'What I see with my eyes,' she answered calmly. 'What I hear with my ears. And … sometimes … things unsaid, things unseen.'

'And how do you do that?' demanded Jodie.

'I listen to the silence between words. I see what people say with their faces, when their tongues utter words which are different.'

'What are you?' asked Adam. 'Some kind of mystic?'

Kali shrugged. 'Perhaps,' she said lightly. 'Who knows?'

'What do you know about my Crystal?' asked Jodie.

Kali trailed her scarf through her fingers. It glittered in the pale afternoon sunlight. 'That it is

indeed unique,' she said. 'That there is some power contained in it.'

'So *you* have it,' said Jodie. 'Why did you take it?'

'In order to return it to you,' she said. 'I believed if I did not take it then some other might do so, and it would be lost to you for ever.'

Jodie sighed with relief. 'Where is it?' he asked.

'Before your eyes,' she said, 'as it was all afternoon. Can't you see it?'

Jodie stared at her.

'Her scarf,' Adam said suddenly. He stepped forward and took it from her hand.

Kali laughed in delight. 'Sharp-eyed Adam,' she cried.

Adam's face went pink with pleasure.

'Hide a tree in a forest,' declared Kali, 'and a book in a library.'

She spread her scarf out on a nearby desk. There among the coloured sequins and the little charms, Kali had fastened the Calling Crystal. She untied the fine thread and handed the Crystal to Jodie.

'What power does it have?' She asked him as they made their way home across the main road.

'Unlimited,' he said. 'Even I don't know its full capacity.' He thought fast. He would have to give the other two some kind of explanation, yet he couldn't burden them with the whole truth. They wouldn't believe it anyway.

'My father was a famous scientist,' Jodie told them. 'He gave me this to keep it safe. The world is not yet ready for it.' He paused. 'There is someone who is trying to take it from me. Someone who lives near here, but I don't know their identity. It may even be that I speak to them every day.'

'In the pay of a foreign power,' said Adam excitedly.

'Something like that,' Jodie said in a tired voice. His head was sore again. Someone or something was trying to break into his thoughts.

Kali smiled into Jodie's eyes. 'You frown so much,' she said, 'as if the troubles of the human race rested on your shoulders.'

'In a way they do,' said Jodie wearily.

'No,' said Kali. 'Not on your shoulders alone. You have friends, Adam and I. We will not reveal your secret to anyone, and if you need hep then you only have to ask.'

Jodie watched Adam and Kali as they walked away towards their homes. They didn't really believe his story. Well, maybe Kali did a little. With her Eastern origins she certainly seemed to be more in tune with nature, less frenetic in her thoughts and deeds than her Western classmates. She was sensitive to people's moods, paid attention to their feelings. Jodie longed to be carefree like his friends. He heard them making arrangements to meet in the chip shop later.

Albert was waiting for Jodie as he came in the back door. 'I'd like to see you, Jodie, please,' he said, 'in my office.'

He ushered Jodie into one of the easy chairs set around the coffee table in the corner. Then he went over to the filing cabinet by the window and took out a folder. He placed it on the table between them.

'This is information on your life, Jodie. You may read through it if you wish.'

Jodie shook his head. He had memorized all its contents before he had left Dijan.

Albert sighed. 'There are some things I would like to discuss with you. Perhaps you might wish to wait until I can call in a Social Worker?'

'No,' said Jodie. He knew that would mean a lot of questions and perhaps a close examination of his past records.

'I didn't think so,' said Albert. He eyes narrowed and he tapped Jodie's folder with his long index finger. 'I've looked through your file myself Jodie, and some of it doesn't seem to fit together.' He paused. 'I think you know what I mean.'

Jodie felt his face colour hotly.

'Yes,' said Albert softly, 'I thought so. You're not like the rest of the children here at all, are you?'

Then, as Jodie still did not reply, Albert said, 'I know exactly what you are.'

CHAPTER NINE

Jodie gulped.

So. This was it. He would die rather than give up his Calling Crystal. He tried to prepare himself. He drew, as best he could, all his reserves of mental energy into one force of resistance.

Albert laughed out loud.

'Don't look so fierce,' he said. 'I can help you. I've dealt with runaways before.'

'Runaways?' said Jodie.

'Yes. That's what you are, isn't it?' said Albert. 'A runaway.'

'A runaway,' Jodie repeated stupidly.

Albert got up and walked round to sit beside Jodie.

'Look, don't worry. I'm going to have to speak to someone in authority quite soon, but we'll work something out. I knew you had problems from the moment you arrived and I'm not usually wrong. But I think it's good for you being here, and you're certainly the best thing that's happened to Beanie for ages. You should have heard him this afternoon, going on about a green furry Kamar. He really believes it, you know. It's great to expand a child's imagination.' Albert patted Jodie on the shoulder. 'Try to talk a bit more. I'm always here for you. Remember that.'

Jodie walked upstairs to his room. He had used a tiny amount of extrasensory perception to verify that Albert was quite genuine in his concern for him. So he could eliminate him as a suspect. But now... having done that, Jodie knew what would happen. The watcher in the shadows would have tracked on to that brief flicker of telepathy. Hardly had he put his school bag down and sat on the edge of his bed than the thoughts came crowding in on him. The Alien was out there, must have felt Jodie's psychic movement and was trying to link up again.

Jodie put his hand to his head. His brain was buzzing. It was being probed, cautiously yet insistently.

He had to make a decision.

It was too dangerous to stay here. The authorities would investigate him and might find out that his family records were all wrong. Soon the Alien would seek him out, find him, take the Crystal and destroy him.

He must leave.

Where could he go? What friends did he have? He thought of Kali and Adam. Perhaps they would help him. He remembered what they had said earlier, about going to the fish and chip shop for supper tonight. Jodie opened his bedroom window softly. He took out the Crystal and keyed in the code to increase its anti-gravity mass. Then, holding it firmly in his hand, he jumped from the window on the grass below.

Kali and Adam and a few other pupils from the school were waiting in the chip shop queue. Jodie walked up to them. 'I need your help,' he whispered urgently.

As they left the shop Mr Neil came in.

'Goodness,' he said. 'Is the whole school having chips for tea tonight?'

'Albert at the Children's Home knows there is something strange about my background,' Jodie told his friends as they walked along the High Street together. 'I cannot stay there any more.' He pressed his hand to his eyes. 'I must tell you the whole truth, although you probably won't believe me.'

Then Jodie told them of his home planet and why he was here on Earth, and of the incident at the power station the night before. As he spoke, Jodie could see the look of disbelief in Adam's eyes. 'I know it's a bit much for you to take in,' he said, 'but I cannot manage on my own any more. My head aches all the time. I can feel the Alien close to me. I am weakening. I cannot resist the pressure much longer.'

Kali put her hand on his arm. 'We will help you,' she said.

'Yeah,' said Adam. 'Tell us who it is, and I'll sort them out.'

'That's the problem,' said Jodie. 'I don't know who it is.'

'**SOON YOU WILL KNOW**,' said a voice distinctly in his ear. '**I AM COMING FOR YOU**.'

Jodie turned round in panic. The street behind them was crowded with tea-time shoppers and workers going home.

'What is it?' said Kali in alarm as she saw the expression on Jodie's face.

'It's here,' said Jodie. 'It spoke to me, right inside my head.' He glanced desperately about him.

'Look!' Adam pointed. 'There's the amusement arcade. You told us electrical impulses confuse energy waves. Let's go in and see if there's a back exit.'

The noise in the darkened arcade was deafening. Adam had been right. The whirring, bleeping machines with their flashing lights and their sudden surges of energy were a mask behind which Jodie's mind could hide. They moved quickly towards the fire exit doors at the rear.

Jodie put his hand on the push bar.

'You kids get away from that door,' a voice called loudly.

They all turned together. It was the security attendant.

'Clear off,' he said rudely, 'and don't let me catch you here again.'

They moved away among the machines. As he glanced back, Jodie could see the attendant standing in front of the door, blocking their way of escape. It would take the Alien only minutes to realize where he had gone. He was trapped! Jodie looked towards the entrance and saw a dark shadow looming outside the main door. Kali and Adam saw it too.

'I have an idea,' said Kali. 'Come. Hurry.' She indicated the small corridor where the toilets were. 'Let's change clothes,' she said to Jodie. 'We are of the same size. They should fit. Then anyone watching the doors will not recognize you as you leave. Adam, stand in front, please, to screen us.' She began to unwrap her sari.

When they had finished, she wound her scarf around Jodie's head, covering his face. 'Now walk slowly alongside Adam,' she said. 'Keep your mind serene.' She touched his face with her fingers. 'Be strong,' she said.

As Jodie turned away, it struck him that it was the second time that her Eastern dress had come to his aid.

Kali waited nearly twenty minutes to let them get clear before she ventured out into the street.

'I hope he got away,' she whispered to herself, as she stepped back into the sunlight wearing Jodie's

jeans and jacket.

Suddenly her wrist was gripped by a hard cruel hand.

'He may have done,' a voice beside her said harshly. 'But you have not!'

CHAPTER TEN

Jodie followed Adam through the back streets and lanes of the town until they came to the flats.

'Take smaller steps,' Adam hissed at him. 'You're striding along like the BFG. Kali walks much more daintily than that.'

They went up in the lift to Adam's flat.

'Let's see if I can find you jeans and a sweatshirt,' he said, rummaging in his wardrobe.

Adam's mobile rang as Jodie was changing. Adam answered it and then, with a puzzled look, gave the phone to Jodie.

'It's Kali,' he said. 'She wants to speak to you.'

'Is she OK?'

'I don't know,' said Adam in a worried voice. 'She sounds scared.'

Jodie took the phone. 'Kali?' he said.

'Jodie, it's the Alien,' Kali's voice was low and urgent. 'Do you understand me, Jodie? The A-L-I-E-N.'

The phone was pulled from Kali's grasp.

'IT IS I.' A rasping voice sound on the line. **'I HAVE THE GIRL. COME WITH THE CRYSTAL TO THE POWER STATION.'**

'Wait!' cried Jodie.

He was too late. There was nothing there. 'It was the Alien,' he told Adam in a shaky voice. 'It has captured Kali and I must exchange the Crystal for her.'

'Did you recognize who it was?' asked Adam.

'No, yet I'm sure I've heard it before,' said Jodie, 'and recently. But it sounded different.' He looked at Adam helplessly. 'I can't go to the police. They would never understand, and if I do Kali will be killed. I must go to the power station with the Crystal.'

'It had to happen,' said Adam. 'You would have

been tracked down eventually. But perhaps we can think of something, some way to outwit...' He stopped and stared at Jodie's neck.

Jodie followed his gaze down. He still had Kali's scarf draped around him.

Jodie fingered its silken folds. 'Ah, yes,' he said.

It was almost dark when Jodie reached the power station. He barely touched the gate with his fingers and it swung open. Jodie started to walk towards the centre of the plant.

'Jodie,' a voice called after him.

Jodie turned. Mr Neil, his teacher, was standing by the gate.

'Jodie,' he called again. 'Come out of there. That isn't a place you should be at night.'

Jodie was so surprised to see his teacher that he took a few steps towards him. Then he stopped. Why was Mr Neil here?

As if he had read his thought, his teacher said casually, 'I was walking my dog in the park and I saw you pass by. Come on. I don't know what you are doing but you must go home now.' He turned away.

A feeling of relief passed of Jodie. Obviously his teacher couldn't be the Alien, by the casual way he was acting, and the fact that he was prepared to move away from the energy field. He ran to catch up with him.

'Are you in some kind of trouble?' Mr Neil asked. 'Can I be of any assistance?'

He would hardly believe it if I told him, thought Jodie, but the helpless feeling inside him seemed to have gone. Perhaps telling an adult at least part of the story would help.

'Kali has been taken away by someone who

wants something of mine,' he gabbled out. 'I had to bring it here and exchange it for her.'

Mr Neil raised his eyebrows.

'Really, Jodie. What could you possible have of value that anyone would want? Gold? Jewels?' He laughed.

'Oh, the Crystal is more important than precious metals or stones,' said Jodie.

'Is it?' said Mr Neil in an interested voice. 'May I see this Calling Crystal?'

'Actually,' Jodie began, 'I …'

He stopped. With absolute horror Mr Neil's last words registered in his mind. 'Calling Crystal' he had said. Yet Jodie knew that he himself had not used that phrase. At the same moment another thought occurred to him.

'Where is your dog?' he asked.

'Dog?' said his teacher. 'What dog?'

'The dog you were walking in the park when you noticed me passing by,' said Jodie nervously. He took a few steps back.

'Mmmm …' Mr Neil smiled in a crafty way. 'Clever. Clever.' His voice had become harsh and guttural. 'Clever little boy. Though not so clever as to see who I was earlier, despite a most obvious clue.'

His voice was taunting as he came towards Jodie. Part of Jodie's brain realised the danger he was in, but he stood as though hypnotized, unable to move.

'You will give me the Crystal!' Mr Neil stretched out his hand to Jodie. His arm was extended, his fingers pointed, and Jodie felt his own will weakening as he stared at it. 'Had your father trained you better, you pathetic Dijan, you would have recognized me earlier. You GuardRings, who claim to have the best minds in the galaxy, who threaten my very existence with your peaceful ways, cannot work out a simple word riddle.' He laughed scornfully, and it seemed to Jodie that he grew in size and loomed above him.

Jodie opened his mouth but no sound came out.

'Stupid Dijan Traveller,' said the mocking voice, 'you must be such a disappointment to your people.' The shadow over Jodie had increased, shutting out all light from the moon and the distant street lamps. 'Don't you remember?' the voice went on. 'I even introduced myself to you. "Mr Neil," I said,

"Mr A. Neil". It is actually written on your classroom door. Teacher "A. NEIL". All you had to do was put the "A" at the end and read it backwards.'

How could I have been so dull? thought Jodie. Kali had tried to tell him on the telephone when she had sounded out the letters. And how easily he'd been fooled by Mr Neil's unconcerned manner at the gate. Deceived by him walking away in the direction of the park, by his apparent disinterest in being near the power station.

Mr Neil stepped forward. His face was only inches from Jodie's.

'Shall I say it for you,' he demanded, 'so that there is no mistake?'

And the darkness spread out over Jodie, cold and without hope, and inside his head he felt another mind probing.

And the word ALIEN! sounded like a scream of terror in his brain.

CHAPTER ELEVEN

The shock of the dark figure lunging towards him brought Jodie to life. With a great effort he flung himself sideways and rolled across the ground. The Alien's hand brushed past his face.

Jodie got to his knees, focussing all his energy on keeping hold of the Crystal. The Alien's will was strong, and with difficulty Jodie stood up. He grasped the Crystal tightly and moved backwards.

STOP!

And then Jodie's mind was filled with noise. A jangling and screeching which jarred his nerves, and below that the deep throb of something else, like the sounding of a drum. A steady low beat. He must resist. He would need all his father's training if he was to succeed tonight. He began to run.

STOP!

The cry came again. More forcefully, more demanding.

Jodie lifted his head and concentrated hard to shut out the interference. It seemed to settle a little, and all the electronic vibrations faded slightly. Immediately he felt calmer, more in control. Using his own will power he closed a section of his mind off and tried to push the Alien's mind away from the active side of his brain. He had to remember the plan he and Adam had made together earlier, and his own part in it. But, he mustn't think about it too clearly. The Alien was tracking his thoughts, was so close beside him, almost like his own shadow which he could never shake off. Jodie gave his recall memory the gentlest of prods to bring it lightly and vaguely to the back of his consciousness. Just a filmy image to keep him right. He settled it in place. And now … he had to send out his own interference to confuse the ESP waves coming at him.

He began to speak aloud.

'There once was a Kamar of Kroo,
Who lived ...'

'Stop, boy! Stop!'

Jodie ignored the shout and ran on, weaving among the power units, following his instinct as to the right direction. He was heading to the central generator where he and Adam had agreed to meet. He reckoned he now knew the reason that the Alien wanted the Crystal handed over in the power station. Although unsure of the complete potential of his Calling Crystal he was aware that it could be linked to other power sources, and could control them. His computer was one example. So, if the Alien gained possession of the Crystal and linked it to the electrical power of the substation ... Jodie shivered as he imagined the damage it could cause.

He had to keep running. Had to keep talking.

'There once was a Kamar of Kroo...' he muttered.

The drum was louder, the blood pounding in his ears. And it was saying something, speaking to him, loudly, firmly, cutting through his babbling.

'The Crystal. The Crystal,' it said.

'… all alone in the zoo, all alone in the zoo …'
Jodie repeated the line again and again, trying to send out gibberish, anything to mask his real intentions.

But still it came, even louder now, and deeper, vibrating inside him, like a heartbeat in his head.

'The Crystal. The Crystal.'

Jodie stopped. Had he made a wrong turning? Which way to go? He looked around him wildly, and plunged on. He wanted to be as close to the main power source as possible, so that he could use it to fight the Alien.

'The Crystal. The Crystal.'

Jodie looked up. He could see the switching gear ahead of him.

The noise was thundering inside him, the sound so loud that he could not contain it.

'The Crystal. The Crystal.'

His ears and brain were going to burst, all at the same time.

'The Crystal. The Crystal.'

He made a few steps forwards, and sent out a tentative message.

'Adam?'

'No!' said a voice behind him. 'Kali!'

Jodie turned. Mr Neil was standing there. He had Kali by the arm.

Mr Neil opened his mouth, and the words were a searing pain inside Jodie's head.

'The Crystal, The Crystal.'

He held out his hand.

Jodie put his own hands over his ears. It was too much. He couldn't stand the pain any more.

'The Crystal…'

Suddenly it stopped. There was a profound and beautiful silence. Jodie opened his eyes. Peace flooded inside him.

Mr Neil was just in front of him. The kindly teacher who always helped Jodie with his work.

'Give me the Crystal, Jodie,' he said in a coaxing voice.

'I…I…don't…' stammered Jodie.

'No!' A small determined figure pushed between them. It was Kali. 'Don't give it to him, Jodie!' she cried. 'Don't give it to him!'

Mr Neil smiled an awful smile.

'No. Don't give it to me, Jodie,' he said. He pulled Kali close to him and grabbed her by the throat. 'Don't give it to me, and … I will kill her.'

CHAPTER TWELVE

Jodie glanced behind him. Only a few paces to go and he would be there, where Adam waited. He backed away slowly.

'Stop!' Mr Neil shouted once more. 'This is the last time I will speak to you.' He tightened his grip on Kali. 'Hand over your Crystal, or I will choke all life from her.'

Jodie gazed at Kali's dark eyes. 'Adam,' he thought silently, 'I hope you are near me now.' He put his hand into the pocket of his jeans.

'All right,' he said. 'Let her go, and I will give it to you.'

'No,' said the Alien. 'First you hand over the Crystal, *then* I will let her go.'

Jodie drew the small star shape from his pocket and held it high above his head. It gleamed white in the moonlight.

'I'm going to throw it to you,' he said, 'and as I do so Kali must run to me.'

The Alien slackened its grip from Kali's neck. It knew that it was about to win. Jodie felt the full surge of its energy field coming towards him. He must act at once before he was completely swamped.

'Hurry, boy,' the Alien snarled, 'or else I will reach out and take it against your will.'

Jodie raised his arm, and, with all his strength, he threw the little star as far away from him as he possible could.

'No!' wailed Kali.

The Alien pushed her aside and she stumbled forwards and fell to the ground.

Jodie raced to her and took her hand.

'Come on,' he cried. 'We must find Adam.'

'But he has the Crystal,' sobbed Kali. 'Mr Neil has the Crystal.'

Jodie bent close to her ear. 'No,' he said softly.

'He has a little silver star-shaped charm from your scarf.'

Kali lifted her face to Jodie. 'My scarf …?' she said.

'Yes,' said Jodie, hauling her to her feet. 'Now we must find Adam before our trick is discovered.'

Kali scrambled to her feet.

'Adam knows what to do,' gasped Jodie as they ran together. 'You and he will have to manage without me. In a few seconds Mr Neil will realize what has happened and he will seek to discover our plan and destroy me. He will be very angry and very powerful.' Jodie's voice shook slightly. 'I'm going to try to close down all my thought processes and only keep my body functioning in order to defend myself.'

As he spoke there came a screech of rage behind them.

Jodie bit his lip. The Alien must have already picked up the star which he and Adam had earlier cut from Kali's scarf. He had hoped to have more time.

'Adam!' he shouted out loud. And as he did so, a blackness came down upon him, shutting out all light and all thought.

'Here I am,' called Adam's voice. He stepped

out from where he had been hiding. 'Over here.'

But Jodie was no longer capable of hearing him.

'This way.' Kali pulled on Jodie's sleeve, then she stopped. 'What's the matter?' she asked. 'What's wrong?'

Jodie turned his face to her but did not reply. His eyes bulged from his head.

'The Crystal,' he mumbled. 'The Crystal.'

With all her might Kali dragged on his arm, pushing and pulling until they reached Adam.

'Is he sick?' asked Adam. 'What's happening?'

'I'm not sure,' said Kali. 'Mr Neil knows he has been fooled. I think he is trying to enter Jodie's mind.'

Every brain cell inside Jodie's head was pulsating in agony. The terrible drumming, throbbing noise which had previously caused him so much pain had increased ten-fold. He tried to escape, turning his thoughts this way and that. But it was no use, he was being pursued like a rat running in a maze. A low moaning came from between his teeth.

'What are we to do?' asked Kali desperately. 'Where is the Crystal?'

Adam's hands were shaking as he took the real

Crystal from his pocket.

'Here it is,' he said. 'Jodie has coded it to explode. I was to take it here, to be beside the main power source. It only needs his thumb print to trigger it, then we will have a little time to get away.'

The two friends looked at each other, and then at Jodie. He was tossing his head from side to side, his eyes rolling in their sockets. His moaning was louder, more like half sobs coming from his lips.

'We must at least try,' said Kali. Her voice trembled. 'That person, Mr Neil, whoever or whatever he is, must never be allowed to control

Jodie's Crystal.'

Adam held out the Crystal and Kali took Jodie's hand in her own. She prised open his thumb and placed it in the centre of the star. Then she hesitated.

'Go on,' said Adam bravely. 'We don't have any other choice.'

Kali pressed Jodie's thumb down. As she did so Jodie's whole body relaxed abruptly. He blinked and his eyes refocused.

'The Crystal?' asked Jodie.

Adam placed the Crystal in plain view on the ground.

'That's what Mr Neil wants,' he declared. 'Let him take it.' He seized Jodie's other arm. 'He'll be here soon. We'd better leave.'

'The Crystal?' Jodie said again.

'Jodie,' Kali whispered. 'I see you are back with us.' She raised her hand and touched his cheek gently. 'Understand this,' she went on. 'Adam has done EXACTLY what you wished.' She quickly put her fingers on his lips. 'Don't say it. Don't even think it. Let us run like the wind.'

CHAPTER THIRTEEN

Jodie, Kali and Adam had hardly reached the first line of trees when the blast from the self-destruct device contained inside the Calling Crystal ripped through the power station.

Jagged red light blazed across the sky followed by an ear-splitting explosion. A rushing wind howled around them and within this terrifying sound the three friends heard the frustrated yell of the alien creature. Then came a tremendous tearing noise as though the sky had been rent apart.

They dived for shelter among the rhododendron bushes.

A massive cloud of smoke billowed out towards them and the acrid smell of burning hung in the air.

They huddled together in silent shock

'That *thing*.' Kali spoke first. 'It won't have been destroyed.' It was a statement rather than a question.

'No,' said Jodie. 'I think the energy impact will have cast it far from Earth's atmosphere into deepest space. But I think it will survive. Survive and perhaps return. I don't know what will happen then,' he added wearily. His struggle with the Alien had left Jodie exhausted.

'By that time we'll be adults,' said Adam. 'We won't make the same mistakes that are being made now. Every day we learn more and more about recycling and conservation and we can start doing things like that right away. '

Kali regarded him curiously.

'Adam …' she said. 'Is that not the name given by some people to the first man on Earth? Perhaps it was meant for you to be here so that we can have a new beginning.'

Adam looked embarrassed. 'It wasn't just me,'

he said. 'We all played a part in this.'

'Yes,' said Jodie. 'We won this battle because the three of us, from different places and peoples, worked together.'

Kali nodded in agreement. 'It's up to each individual to think of their actions that affect us all. Then, united in purpose, we can look after our planet more carefully.'

The arrival of the emergency service vehicles made them move away to the other side of the park.

'What will you do now, Jodie?' Adam asked.

'The Crystal is destroyed.' Jodie's face became serious as the full truth of his predicament struck him. 'I am cut off from Dijan,' he said in a low voice, 'for how long I don't know.'

'You could hide out in an empty house. We could bring you food,' suggested Adam.

Kali shook her head. 'The Children's Home would report you missing. They would search for you everywhere.'

Jodie thought about his situation, considering all the possible options open to him.

'I'll go back to the Children's Home,' he said at last. 'Hopefully the computer records which my father altered will stand investigation. Albert is sympathetic. He thinks that I don't discuss my background because I've been badly-treated in the past. I believe that I will be allowed to stay there.'

He glanced at his friends, Kali and Adam, and felt comforted. 'It won't be so strange for me now that I have you two who understand. Anyway,' he smiled, 'I have lots more Dijan limericks to tell Beanie, and he might be able to teach me how to play football. And…'

Jodie looked up at the stars which were starting to twinkle in the night sky.

'…Some day my father will come for me.'

Author Biography

Theresa Breslin was born near Glasgow and has lived there all her life. Many of her books have a Scottish setting. The trilogy about Kezzie set during World War 2, REMEMBRANCE about World War 1 and DIVIDED CITY about the Catholic/Protestant split in football loyalties in the West of Scotland. Theresa won the Carnegie medal for her novel about a dyslexic boy, WHISPERS IN THE GRAVEYARD. More recently she has written two historical novels, THE MEDICI SEAL about Leonardo Da Vinci and THE NOSTRADAMUS PAPERS .

Before becoming a writer, Theresa was a children's librarian, She has four children and numerous grandchildren and lives with her husband, a former teacher, near Glasgow.